SPOTLIGHT ON SOCCER

SOCCER RULES AND REGULATIONS

Clive Gifford

PowerKiDS
press™

New York

Published in 2011 by The Rosen Publishing Group Inc.
29 East 21st Street, New York, NY 10010

Copyright © 2011 Wayland/
The Rosen Publishing Group, Inc.

First Edition

Editor: Julia Adams
Produced by: Tall Tree Ltd.
Editor, Tall Tree: Jon Richards
Designer: Ben Ruocco

Library of Congress Cataloging-in-Publication Data

Gifford, Clive.
  Soccer rules and regulations / by Clive Gifford. -- 1st ed.
      p. cm. -- (Spotlight on soccer)
  Includes index.
  ISBN 978-1-61532-608-2 (library binding)
  ISBN 978-1-61532-613-6 (paperkback)
  ISBN 978-1-61532-617-4 (6-pack)
  1. Soccer--Rules--Juvenile literature. I. Title.
  GV943.4.G55 2011
  796.334--dc22

                              2009045781

4616 8901 5/11

Photographs
All photographs taken by Michael Wicks, except;
t—top, l—left, r—right, b—bottom, c—center
cover t—Dreamstime.com/Jimsphotos, tr—Dreamstime.
com/Photosfromafrica, br—Dreamstime.com/Ivz,
bl—Dreamstime.com/Ivz, tl—Dreamstime.com/Rcyoung,
c—Dreamstime.com/Lariotus, 1 Dreamstime.com/Dong
Hj, 4 Dreamstime.com/Ivan Tykhyi, 5 Dreamstime.com/
Daniele Morra, 6 istockphoto.com/Duncan Walker, 7t
Dreamstime.com/Shariff Che' Lah, 7b Dreamstime.com/
Dmitry Argunov, 8 Dreamstime.com/Duncan Walker, 10
Dreamstime.com/Ivan Tykhyi, 12 Dreamstime.com/Steve
Woods, 13b Dreamstime.com/Ami Levin, 15 Dreamstime.
com/Igor Zhorov, 17b Dreamstime.com/Matt Trommer, 18
Dreamstime.com/Lario Tus, 20 Dreamstime.com/Mitchell
Gunn, 21 Andres Stapff/Reuters/Corbis, 22 Sampics/Corbis,
23 Dreamstime.com/Dong Hj, 29 Srdjan Suki/epa/Corbis,
30 Rafael Diaz/epa/Corbis, 32 Dreamstime.com/Ivan Tykhyi

Acknowledgements
The author and publisher would like to thank the
following people for their help and participation in this
book: Whiteknights FC, Eric Burrow, Steve Rendell, and
Paul Scholey.

Manufactured in China.
CPSIA Compliance Information: Batch #WAS0102PK: For Further Information contact
Rosen Publishing, New York, New York at 1-800-237-9932

CONTENTS

The Game's Rules

Soccer is an exciting and dynamic team ball sport. The game is played according to a set of rules, or laws, that are reviewed regularly by the sport's governing bodies.

Why Does Soccer Need Rules?

Without rules to tell players how to play, soccer could turn into a chaotic and dangerous game. The rules were created to protect the players from risky play and to make the game exciting to play. They also help to make the game fun to watch so that people keep coming to support teams at stadiums around the world and watch games on television.

ON THE BALL

Before 1891, referees did not have to be in charge of matches. Instead, players would control the games themselves, or pick a pair of umpires, one from each team.

Ismaël Bangoura (in white) of Guinea shoots at the goal while playing for the Ukrainian team Dynamo Kiev against the English club, Arsenal. Players score goals by putting the ball into the opposing team's net using any part of their body, except for their hands and arms.

Rules of the Game

Soccer's key rules are collected in a booklet called *Laws of the Game*. There are a total of 17 laws in the booklet and these cover all aspects of the game, from the size of the field to the players' equipment, and from misconduct to the methods of scoring goals. A team of officials on the field oversees matches and makes sure that players follow these laws.

A goalkeeper stretches up to catch a high ball. Law 3 from *Laws of the Game* states that the teams playing a match should contain a minimum of seven players and a maximum of 11, one of whom should be a goalkeeper. The goalkeeper is the only player who can handle the ball on the field.

Early Rules

More than 150 years ago, soccer was a rough game similar to rugby, with players grabbing and pulling each other as they wrestled for the ball. The first rules were drawn up in the mid-nineteenth century by teams from British private schools and universities.

Rule Changes

Members of many early British soccer teams met in London in 1863 to form the Football (Soccer) Association and draw up a set of rules. Over time, these became *Laws of the Game.* The rules were basic at first. Until 1891, many soccer matches were played without a crossbar on top of the goalposts. Until 1913, goalkeepers were allowed to grab the ball anywhere in their own half of the field.

ON THE BALL

In the early days, each English school had its own rules. At Harrow School, for example, a tie game was replayed the following day with the goals made twice as wide!

These English schoolboys are wearing caps and heavy shoes to play soccer in around 1900. According to the original laws of 1863, players were not allowed to wear shoes with metal plates or nails that stuck out from the soles.

Versions of the Game

Although today's rules deal with the full version of soccer, there are many different versions of soccer that are played under their own rules. These include futsal, which is played by teams made up of just five players on an indoor field that is smaller than a full-size soccer field. The goal is also smaller—just 6.5 feet (2 m) high by 9.8 feet (3 m) wide.

Russian team VIZ-Sinara (in white) scores a goal against Italian Luparense (in blue) during a futsal match. As well as having fewer players and a smaller field, futsal is played with a lighter and smaller ball than in the full version of the game.

A player is carried off on a stretcher during a match between China and Myanmar. Today, a substitute can take the injured player's place, but this was not allowed before the 1950s. Before this, the injured player's team would continue playing with just ten soccer players.

The Rulemakers

Soccer's rules are regularly altered and new rules are talked about and tested. Any new rule has to be approved by the International Football (Soccer) Association Board (IFAB).

Making the Laws

The IFAB is made up of eight representatives—four from FIFA and one from each of the UK's soccer associations (England, Scotland, Northern Ireland, and Wales). The board meets twice a year to study and vote on any rule changes. Each representative has one vote and rule changes are passed only if they win at least six votes.

Natasha Kai (in white) of the United States celebrates scoring against Canada. She makes sure that she does not get too carried away with her celebration so that she is not punished by the referee.

Modern Rule Changes

The IFAB changes rules in order to make the game safer for players and more exciting for people to watch. For instance, the backpass rule was introduced in 1992 and was designed to reduce time-wasting. It means that a goalkeeper cannot handle the ball when it is passed back deliberately by a teammate. Instead, the goalkeeper must kick or head the ball. In the 1990s and 2000s, players scoring a goal often made elaborate goal celebrations. Referees will now caution any player who is guilty of time-wasting when celebrating a goal. During the 2006 World Cup, Carlos Tévez of Argentina and Arjen Robben of Holland were both shown a yellow card for jumping into the crowd while celebrating scoring a goal.

RULE SCHOOL
When the referee signals a foul against your team, do not argue or hold onto the ball or you might be cautioned for dissent (arguing) or time-wasting. Run back into position to help your team defend.

This goalkeeper is hurrying to kick the ball clear after a pass from a teammate. Before the 1992 law change concerning the backpass, she could have picked the ball up, but since this has now been banned, an attacker (shown here in blue) can rush in to challenge the keeper, hoping to force a mistake.

The Rule Enforcers

Major soccer matches are run by four officials. The referee has ultimate control over the game. There are also two assistants who run the touchlines and the fourth official who helps with several duties.

A Referee's Role

Referees make all decisions during a match, from whether a goal has been scored to whether a foul has been committed. They have to be fit so that they can keep up with play during a fast-moving match. They may have to run 6 miles (10 km) in a match. A referee also has many duties before and after a game, including filing a detailed report on the match. During the game, they are in charge of timekeeping, deciding when the match starts and stops.

Spanish referee Luis Medina Cantalejo warns players during a Champions League match in 2008. Referees need to spot any law infringements and keep players under control.

RULE SCHOOL
The referee's decision is final and players should never argue with or insult the referee. Particularly violent insults or arguments with a referee can see a player banned for many games.

Referee's Signals

This is the signal for an indirect free kick. Players who are awarded an indirect free kick cannot shoot directly at goal, but must pass to a teammate first.

This is the signal for a direct free kick. Players who are awarded a direct free kick can shoot directly at goal.

This referee has awarded a penalty for a serious offense or foul that has taken place inside the penalty area. He is pointing directly at the penalty spot.

Other Officials

The referee is helped by a pair of assistants who run each sideline and signal when the ball goes out of play. Assistant referees signal when offside occurs, or when a team wants to make a substitution. They can also advise the referee about a serious foul when the referee does not have a good view. Assistant referees carry flags that they use to communicate with the referee. The fourth official is also on the sidelines, assisting the referee with certain tasks. These include holding up a sign to show how much time is added on at the end of a match, looking after replacement balls, and helping when a substitute is made. They can also take the place of an injured official.

> " *I know I have to be good as [since] others may get a chance. It is not easy because I am judged more harshly than a man, and any mistakes are attributed solely to the fact that I am a woman.* "
>
> **Nicole Petignat**, the first female referee of a Union of European Football Associations (UEFA) match

Start and Finish

A full game of soccer lasts for 90 minutes. It is divided up into two halves, each lasting 45 minutes, with a 15-minute halftime period. At the start of the second half, teams switch halves, changing the end that they defend. In some competitions, if the score is tied at the end of the 90 minutes, two 15-minute periods of extra time are played.

RULE SCHOOL
If a player wastes time during the minutes of added on time at the end of a half, the referee can caution the player and add on extra time.

Winning the Toss

A game of soccer starts with the kickoff. This sees one of the teams play the ball from the center spot in the middle of the field, while opposition players stand outside the center circle (see page 13). Just before the start of a match, the teams will decide which end they will defend and who should take the kickoff. This is usually decided with the toss of a coin by the referee. The team that guesses correctly gets to choose which end to defend or if they want to take the kickoff. Kickoffs are also used to restart a game after a goal has been scored.

The Kickoff

1 When teams line up for the kickoff, only players from the team kicking off (in blue) are allowed inside the center circle. Opposition players (in yellow) must stand outside.

2 One of the players in the team kicking off will take responsibility for the first touch. He must move the ball forward, otherwise the referee will award a free kick to the opposition.

3 After the first kick, the second touch must be made by another player. He can pass the ball in any direction.

Open Play

After the kickoff, the game continues all over the field. This is called open play. Play continues until one of the following happens: the ball leaves the field and is out of play, a goal is scored, a foul or serious injury occurs, the referee stops play for an unexpected incident, such as a field invasion by fans, or the ball is damaged. If the game is stopped with the ball still in open play, the referee restarts the game with a drop ball— dropping the ball between a player from each side. The two players cannot compete for the ball or touch it until it hits the ground.

Toward the end of each half of the match, the fourth official will hold up an electronic sign showing how many minutes are added on to the end of a match due to injuries and other stoppages.

ON THE BALL

At the 1990 World Cup semifinal between Italy and Argentina, referee Michel Vautrot forgot to check the time and accidentally added eight extra minutes of play.

In or Out?

Many decisions in soccer involve officials determining whether the ball was in or out of play. The ball is in play when it is on the field, and out of play when it has crossed the lines marking the field boundary.

Over the Line

In order for a ball to be out of play, it has to cross the lines marking the edge of the field completely. If any part of the ball is touching the lines, then it is still in play. This also applies to when a goal is scored. A goal is awarded when the entire ball crosses the goal line between the two goalposts. When the ball has gone out of play, the game is restarted by a throw-in if the ball crossed a sideline. If the ball crossed the goal line outside of the goalposts, then the game is restarted with a goal kick if an attacker was the last player to touch the ball. If a defender was the last person to touch the ball, then the attacking team is awarded a corner kick.

Out of play

In play

If any part of the ball is on the edge of a sideline or goal line, it is still in play.

RULE SCHOOL
You are allowed to score a goal directly from a corner, without the ball touching another player. However, you cannot score directly from a throw-in.

Restarting

There are several laws to follow when taking throw-ins and corners. If a player commits a foul throw (see right), then the opposition is awarded the throw-in. For a corner, the ball must be placed inside a quadrant on the side of the field where the ball went out of play. If a player fails to follow the laws regarding taking a corner, then the opposition is awarded a free kick.

This player has stepped over the sideline with both feet while taking a throw-in. A referee would also award a foul throw if he had stepped over the line with just one foot.

This player has taken one hand off the ball while throwing in. Foul throws are also awarded when the player does not take the ball back behind his head or if he has one foot in the air.

Wesley Sneijder of the Spanish club Real Madrid prepares to take a corner. A corner-taker cannot kick the ball a second time until another player has touched it.

Fouls

There are many different types of fouls in soccer. A foul may be violent or dangerous play or it could involve holding back a player and stopping them from getting to the ball.

Excessive Contact

Soccer is considered a noncontact sport. In reality, some contact is allowed, but most fouls occur when the referee considers that there has been excessive (too much) contact. These fouls include a player pushing or holding another player, jumping or charging at an opponent, or when a player attempts to make a tackle but makes contact with the opponent before touching the ball. A player is guilty of a foul if they kick or trip an opponent. Even if they attempt but fail to perform these offenses, the referee can signal a foul.

Alexandru Gatcan of Moldova (in blue) collides with Luka Modric of Croatia, committing a foul. In some cases, even if a serious foul like this has happened, the referee will signal for play to continue if the team that has been fouled is in a good position. This is called playing advantage.

18

Dangerous tackling is one of the most important issues in football [soccer] at the moment. Players who do this kind of thing intentionally should be banned from the game.

FIFA President,
Sepp Blatter

Other Offenses

Dangerous play is considered a foul. This is when, for example, a player lifts their foot high to try to kick the ball when it is near an opponent's head. Handball is a foul and occurs when a player deliberately lets an arm or hand connect with the ball. However, when the ball is kicked from one or two yards away straight at an opponent's arm, the referee rarely signals handball. Obstruction is when a player not playing the ball stops an opponent from getting past by blocking their path.

The defender (in yellow) is pulling on the attacker's shirt and holding her back. If the attacker was in the penalty area, then the referee could award the attacker a penalty (see pages 28–29) for being held back from a goal-scoring opportunity.

Misconduct

A number of offenses are grouped together and called misconduct. These have to be judged by the referee, who may issue red or yellow cards.

Misconduct

Players are guilty of misconduct if, for example, they deliberately delay the game being restarted. They can do this by holding onto the ball when it should go to the other team or by standing in front of where a free kick is to be taken and not retreating the required distance. Dissent is refusing to accept a referee's decision or arguing with the match officials. For all of the above offenses, a referee is likely to caution the players and show them a yellow card (see pages 22–23).

> *Referees and players have got to trust each other. We are not enemies, we just do our jobs in different ways.*
>
> Italian referee,
> **Pierluigi Collina**

Match officials step in to stop players from English clubs Chelsea and Manchester United arguing. In these situations, officials need to act quickly to prevent any violent behavior.

Álvaro Recoba of Uruguay takes off his shirt while celebrating a goal during a match against Argentina. Such behavior is a misconduct offense and a referee will show the guilty player a yellow card (see pages 22–23).

Violence, Professional Fouls, and Simulation

Soccer players sometimes abuse opponents, spectators, or the referee, fight, spit at another player, or make particularly brutal and dangerous tackles. Such actions break the laws of soccer and are usually punished heavily. Even when a foul is not particularly brutal, it can result in the player being sent off the field because they deliberately denied the other team a clear chance to score a goal. This is known as a professional foul. Simulation is pretending to be fouled and hurt, usually to get an opponent in trouble or to win a penalty or free kick unfairly.

ON THE BALL

At a match at the 2002 World Cup, Brazil's Rivaldo faked being hit in the face by a ball kicked by an opponent. After the match, Rivaldo was fined 11,670 Swiss francs ($11,400).

Red and Yellow

A referee can punish players by showing them a yellow or red card. A yellow card, or booking, cautions a player and warns them about their conduct. A red card indicates that the player has been sent off the field.

Cautions and Sendings Off

Cards are awarded by the referee when a player is guilty of a foul or misconduct. If these are serious enough, the referee cautions the player and shows them a yellow card. Two yellow cards in the same match equal a red card. So, if that player commits another serious foul, the referee will show them a second yellow card, followed by a red. When players are shown a red card, they must leave the field, and their team has to continue with one player less. If a player is guilty of abusive or violent play, the referee may send them straight off the field.

Many players will appeal to the referee to try to change a decision. Here, Bastian Schweinsteiger of the German club, Bayern Munich, pleads with the referee not to book one of his teammates. The pleading failed, as his teammate was sent off the field.

Sent to the Stands

In many competitions, a record is kept of the red and yellow cards collected by a player. In the 2006 World Cup, any player receiving two yellow cards in matches during the early stages of the competition was banned from playing in the next game. Referees can also show cards to players and coaching staff who are standing on the sidelines. At Euro 2008, referee Manuel Mejuto González sent off both the German manager, Joachim Löw, and the Austrian manager, Josef Hickersberger, for arguing with the fourth official. When a manager is sent off, they have to leave the edge of the field, usually to take a seat up in the stadium. A ban from sitting with their team at the side of the field for one or more future games usually follows.

A referee books a Vietnamese defender for holding up play by not retreating enough prior to a free kick being taken in a match against China.

Free Kicks

Free kicks are awarded by referees for fouls, infringements, and misconduct. Teams awarded a free kick may pass or shoot, while opposition players must stand 10 yards (9 meters) away and cannot challenge the first kick.

RULE SCHOOL
Indirect free kicks are sometimes awarded deep inside an opponent's penalty area. Defenders can stand on the goal line, even if they are less than 10 yards (9 m) away from the free kick.

Direct and Indirect

There are two types of free kick: direct and indirect. A direct free kick allows a team to shoot directly at the goal with the first kick of the ball. An indirect free kick requires the ball to be touched once by one player before another player can shoot. Direct free kicks are awarded when a foul has been committed, such as a trip or push, or for making excessive contact with a player. Indirect free kicks are awarded for technical offenses, such as when a goalkeeper picks up a pass from a teammate (see page 9). Provided that the ball is stationary, teams can take a free kick quickly, while the opposition players are disorganized, or slowly, so that they can plan what to do.

Three attackers discuss their options for a free kick close to the goal. One of them could shoot directly at the goal, or they could pass the ball to one side for a teammate to shoot instead.

The Defending Team

When a free kick is awarded, the players of the defending team have to retreat 10 yards (9 m) immediately. A defender who kicks the ball away or stands in front of a free kick taker to stop them taking the kick may be cautioned by the referee. When a free kick is awarded close to a defending team's goal, the defenders will usually form a wall of three or more players to help protect their goal. The goalkeeper will shout instructions to the players in the wall, telling them exactly where to stand so that they shield part of the goal.

"With a free kick around the penalty area, we always ask the players whether they want it quick or slow. As long as the ball is stationary and in the right place, then the attacking team can take it as quickly as they like.

Former FIFA referee,
Graham Poll

An attacker lines up to shoot a direct free kick. In front of him, three defenders stand close together to form a wall. This should be positioned carefully with the help of the goalkeeper, otherwise the free kick taker may have a clear shot at the goal.

Offside!

The offside rule prevents attacking players from waiting around the opposition goal. It is a very difficult law to judge, because referees and assistants need to be aware of where every player on the field is standing.

The Basic Rule

Players are in an offside position if, at the moment the ball is played, they do not have two of the opposing team between themselves and the other team's goal line. A player who is level with two opponents or with the second-from-last opponent is not offside. When a player is signaled offside, the opposing team gets an indirect free kick from the point where the player was offside.

line of defenders

offside attacker

Here, the attacker in red is in an offside position because they are behind the line of defenders when the pass is made. Players are ruled offside only if they are in "active play," such as drawing a defender or playing the ball.

Exceptions

There are a number of situations where a player may be standing in what looks like an offside position, but the game continues without offside being given. You cannot be offside if you are in possession of the ball, you are in your own half of the field, or if you receive the ball directly from a throw-in, corner kick, or goal kick. This is why an attacker will sometimes sprint toward the opponent's goal after a goal kick. Players can also time their runs so that they are not offside as the ball is kicked, and then run past defenders to collect the ball.

A referee's assistant signals offside by holding out his flag in front of him.

> **An offside may only be... an offense when the ball is played by a teammate... you cannot be judged offside from a pass from the opposition.**
>
> Australian referee,
> **Steve Alexander**

Penalties and Shoot-Outs

A penalty is a free shot by an attacking player that is taken from the penalty spot. A penalty is a great opportunity to score, because the player who takes the penalty has only the keeper to beat.

Taking a Penalty

Penalties are awarded when players in their own penalty area commit a foul or handball for which the referee would normally award a direct free kick. Only two players are allowed inside the penalty area during a penalty—the goalkeeper and the penalty-taker. The penalty-taker places the ball on the penalty spot, 12 yards (11 m) from the goal, takes a run-up, and must kick the ball forward. If a player from the defending team steps into the penalty area before the kick has been made, the referee can order the kick to be retaken if the penalty is missed.

An attacker (in blue) runs up to take a penalty while a teammate and defenders wait outside the penalty area. The goalkeeper must stay on the line until the kick has been made, but he can move along the line between the goalposts.

Penalty Shoot-Out

A penalty shoot-out is a series of penalties used to decide the winner of a match that has ended in a draw. Shoot-outs are usually held at the end of drawn matches in knockout competitions. Five players from each side take a penalty and, if the scores are still even, penalties continue until one side misses and one scores. The pressures on penalty-takers are immense—one mistake and their team could lose the entire match.

Antonio Puerta (in red) of the Spanish team Sevilla scores during a penalty shoot-out in the 2007 UEFA Cup final against Espanyol of Spain. Sevilla won the shoot-out and the game 3–1.

" *I am so sorry for missing the penalty and denying the fans, my teammates, family, and friends the chance to be European champions.* "

Chelsea captain, **John Terry**, on missing a penalty in the shoot-out in the 2008 Champions League final against Manchester United in the UK

RULE SCHOOL
If a penalty shoot-out lasts 11 penalties per team without a winner, then every player in a team has to take a penalty, including the goalkeeper.

What It Takes To Be...

A Referee

Pierluigi Collina

The world's most recognizable referee first took a refereeing course at the age of 18. After completing a degree in economics, Collina rose through the refereeing ranks in Italy and began taking charge of matches in the top two divisions, Serie A and Serie B, from 1991 onward. Considered an outstanding, fair, and accurate official, he was promoted to FIFA's list of referees, which enabled him to referee important club and international matches.

Career Path

- ⚽ 1988: Refereeing Italian Serie C1 and C2 matches.

- ⚽ 1995: Appointed to FIFA's list of referees after just over 40 Serie A matches.

- ⚽ 1996: Refereed Olympic Games soccer final.

- ⚽ 2002: Refereed the final of the FIFA World Cup.

- ⚽ 2003: Voted world's best referee for the sixth time in a row.

- ⚽ 2004: Refereed UEFA Cup final.

Collina stopped refereeing in 2005 when he reached the referees' official retirement age of 45.

Glossary

booking also called a caution, this is when the referee warns a player for dangerous play and shows a yellow card.

corner restarting the game when the ball has gone out of play over the goal line and a defender was the last person to touch the ball.

extra time two periods of 15 minutes each that are added to the end of some matches when they have finished in a draw. Teams swap ends at the end of the first period of extra time.

FIFA (Fédération Internationale de Football Association) the organization that governs soccer around the world.

free kick an uncontested kick awarded to a team after an opposition player commits an offense, such as a foul, dangerous play, or a handball.

halftime a short period, usually of 15 minutes, separating two halves of a match.

kickoff restarting the game from the center spot in the middle of the field, used at the start of each half and after a goal.

noncontact sport a sport that does not rely on players physically stopping or blocking opposition players.

open play continuous play until the ball goes out of play or an offense is committed.

throw-in restarting the game after the ball has gone out of play over one of the sidelines. The ball is thrown back onto the field by a player using both hands.

toss before the match, the referee tosses a coin and the side that guesses heads or tails correctly chooses whether to take the kickoff or which end to defend.

Further Reading

Official Rules of Soccer
by FIFA (Triumph Books, 2006)

Soccer: Rules, Tips, Strategy, And Safety
by Brian Wingate
(Rosen Publishing Group, 2007)

The Everything Kids' Soccer Book
by Deborah W Orisfield
(Adams Media, 2009)

Web Sites

Due to the changing nature of Internet links, PowerKids Press has developed an online list of Web sites related to the subject of this book. This site is updated regularly. Please use this link to access this list:
http://www.powerkidslinks.com/sos/rules

Index

Ah, ko! Beautiful.
And she wiggled and giggled
as little girls do.

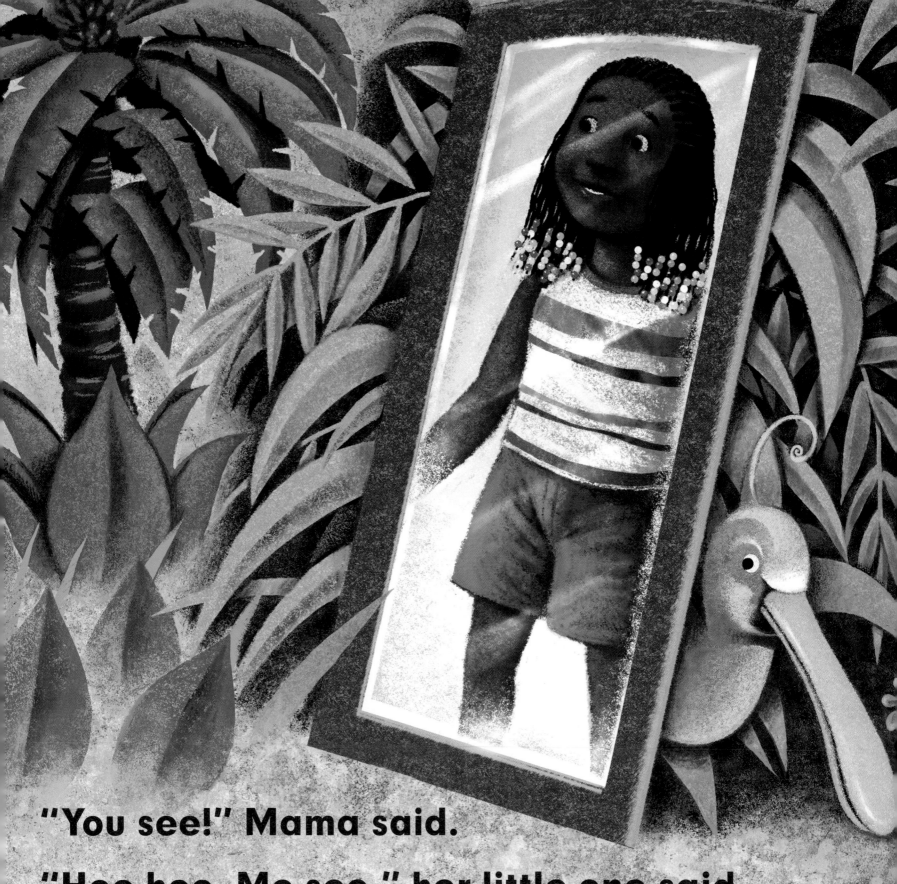

"You see!" Mama said.
"Hee hee. Me see," her little one said.

**Then they came
and stood before their look so selves.**

and into Shemama's arms.

With piney pig's tail, thumb,
and fingers, Shemama made
plait-a-plait and string-a-bead
each one.

Tip pi Tap pi

**The Wild Waiyuuzee
came wee foot and foot
out of the bush . . .**

"Come, come, little one" said Shemama.

"No owie owie me?" asked the Wild Waiyuuzee.

"No owie owie."

"Moka true?"

"Moka true."

But, ah, ko!
Nowhere to go.

TRUMP! TRUMP!

Oh, how the Wild Waiyuuzee
wanted to be still like a rock,
but shook top and bottom
when she heard . . .

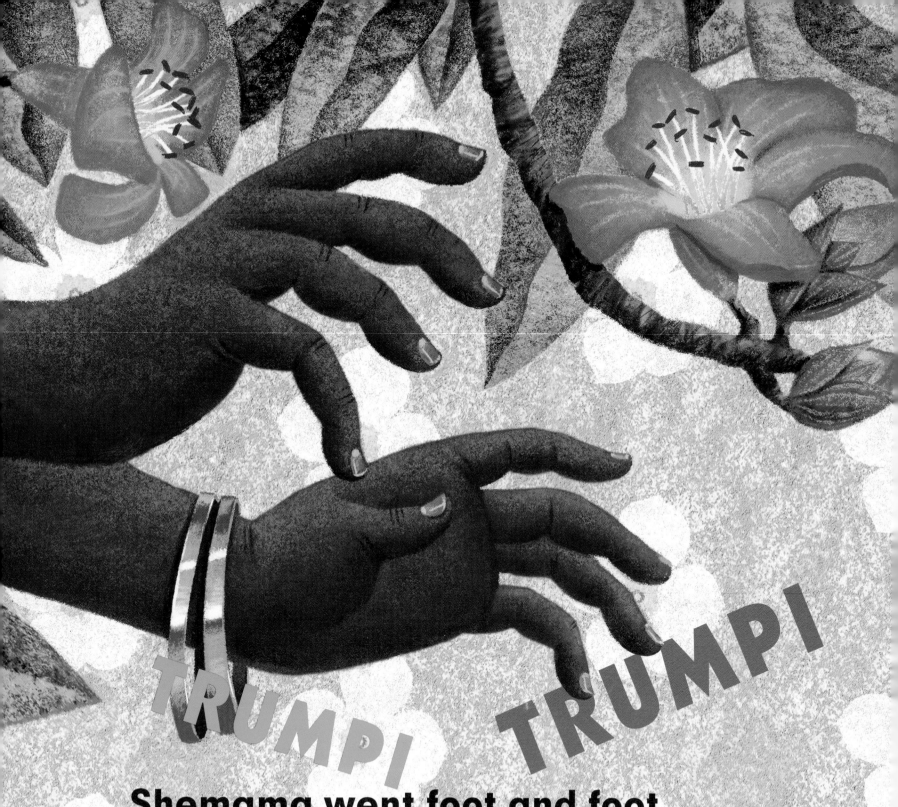

TRUMPI! TRUMPI!

**Shemama went foot and foot
into the bush after the Wild Waiyuuzee.**

"No see. No me,"
cried the Wild Waiyuuzee.

Shemama hopping hot foot now.
"I'm going to comb you with my piney
pig's tail."

"Hee hee. No me," said the Wild
Waiyuuzee.

"Then I'm going to plait-a-plait
and string-a-bead. Wait, you'll see."

back into the bush.

But one good wiggle
and the Wild Waiyuuzee was free.

Off she ran

Tippi Tappi

Tippi Tappi

so Shemama caught that
Wild Waiyuuzee and

PATTI PATTI
RUB RUB

put nut-nut oil on that
nut-nut head.

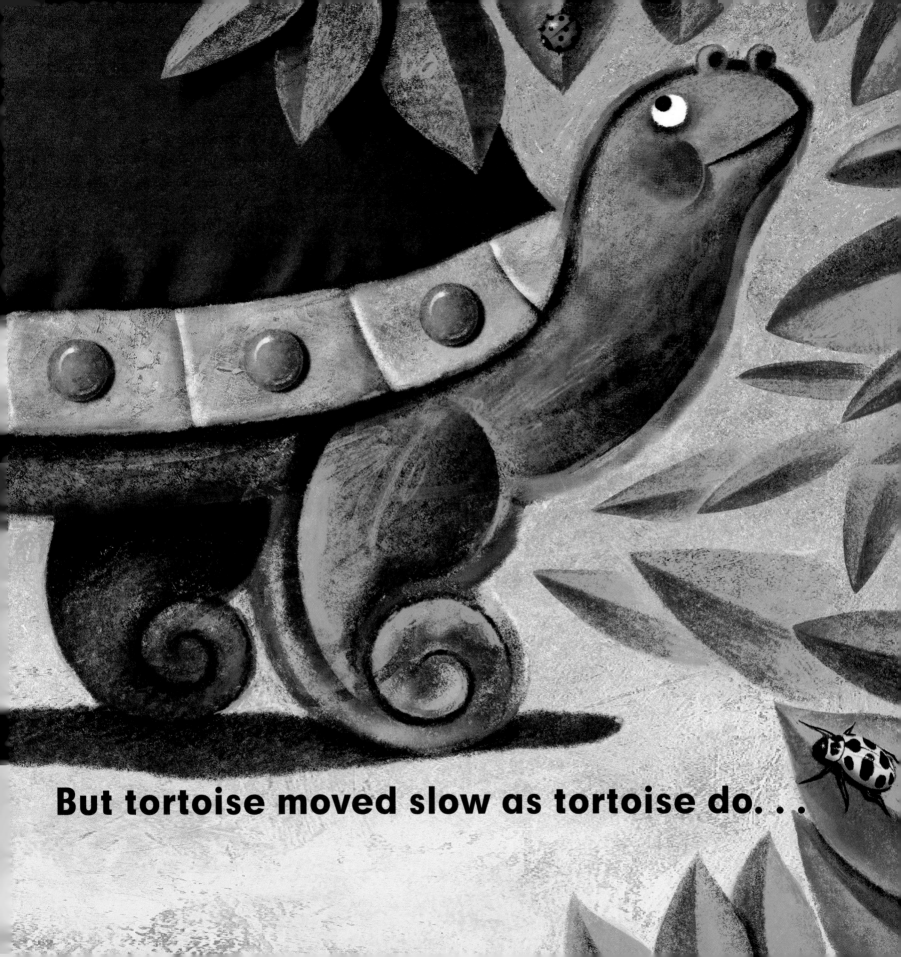

But tortoise moved slow as tortoise do. . . .

"No me! No me!" cried the Wild Waiyuuzee, and she leaped on top of a tortoise shell.

BANG-O-BOK!
BANG-O-BOK!

Shemama started cracking
nut-nuts for nut-nut oil.

Ah, ko!

The very thing needed to
catch a Wild Waiyuuzee.

"I'm going to oil you,
my Wild Waiyuuzee."

All was quiet. All was safe. Until . . .

Wetty wet-wet!

**The Wild Waiyuuzee rolled out
of the high grass and
into
an
iguana
cave.**

Splee-ZASH!

went the water.

Shemama called out,
"I'm going to spray you
with my jumbo sprayer!"

"Eee no! Eee no!" squealed
the Wild Waiyuuzee.

But she stood still like rock,
hoping to trick Shemama.

TRUMPI TRUMPI

Shemama coming foot and foot after the Wild Waiyuuzee.

Oh, how the Wild Waiyuuzee wanted to wiggle and giggle as all Wild Waiyuuzees do.

Tippi Tappi

Tappi Tappi

deep into the mango grove.

Hot on her heels was
Shemama the Catcher calling,
"Wait, you'll see, my Wild
Waiyuuzee."

The Wild Waiyuuzee called
back, "No see, no see," and ran

Out of
the bush ran
the Wild Waiyuuzee.

SIMON & SCHUSTER BOOKS FOR YOUNG READERS An imprint of
Simon & Schuster Children's Publishing Division, 1230 Avenue of the Americas,
New York, New York 10020. Text copyright © 2000 by Rita Williams-Garcia.
Illustrations copyright © 2000 by Mike Reed. All rights reserved including the right
of reproduction in whole or in part in any form. SIMON & SCHUSTER BOOKS FOR YOUNG
READERS is a trademark of Simon & Schuster. Book design by Anahid Hamparian.
    The text for this book is set in Geometric 706. The illustrations were rendered in
    Photoshop. Printed in United States of America   10 9 8 7 6 5 4 3 2 1
LIBRARY OF CONGRESS CATALOGING-IN-PUBLICATION DATA: Williams-Garcia, Rita.
Catching the wlld waiyuuzee / by Rita Williams-Garcia ; illustrated by Mike Reed.
    p. cm. Summary: As she tries to escape her mother's efforts to "plait-a-plait" and
    "string-a-bead" her hair, a young girl imagines herself running away into a jungle.
        ISBN 0-689-82601-X [1. Hair—Fiction. 2. Mothers and daughters—Fiction.
        3. Afro-Americans—Fiction.] I. Reed, Mike, 1951- , ill. II. Title.
        PZ7.W6713 Cat 2000   [E]—dc21   98-49497   CIP AC

first
edition

To Stephanie Elaine,
my own Wild Waiyuuzee
—R. Wms.-G.

To Jane, Alex, and Joe
—M. R.

Catching the Wild Waiyuuzee

Rita Williams-Garcia

illustrated by
Mike Reed

Simon & Schuster Books for Young Readers
NEW YORK   LONDON   TORONTO   SYDNEY   SINGAPORE